The Kid Who Went to the MOON!

by
Walter Levin

THAT'S ONE SMALL STEP for a kid, and one giant leap for kid-kind.

My name is James Gibson, and I've always been fascinated by space travel. All my life, I've been writing to NASA, asking them to send me into space instead of the monkeys they kept sending. When I saw space on TV, I thought it would be cool to go there, since no kid has ever been. But I never really got an answer.

Until one day…I woke up from a nap as my phone buzzed in my back pocket.

My older sister, Sydney, made a face. "Ew! You farted!"

"Did not!" I said.

I checked my phone and thought I was hallucinating. I actually had an email response from NASA! I opened the email to read…a big NO. They also wrote, "Stop emailing us, you bum."

Well, that didn't go too well. But if they thought that their answer would put an end to my dream, they were one hundred percent WRONG. I knew that someday I would go to the moon, or even to another planet.

One morning, Sydney was watching TV—some stupid fashion show with weird people wearing weird things. It was the day of a special on TV that showed Neil Armstrong landing on the moon. This happened back in 1969, and it's always fun to watch it again, especially when it's on TV.

"Sydney," I said, "let me watch the broadcast."

"No," she said. She was really crabby and

wouldn't budge. Let me tell you, sometimes I really wished I was an only child.

My dad was watching the fashion show with her. "Dad," I said, "tell her to move. I need to watch history go by!"

"Sorry, James," he said, not looking away from the screen. "This is important, too."

A few months ago our TV broke, and it was stuck on channel 43 for a few weeks. Channel 43 is the fashion and clothes network, and my dad got hooked on it. He kept watching it even after the TV was fixed, so he was going to be no help to make my sister give me the remote.

I called my mom to come downstairs and tell my sister and my dad to let me watch the news broadcast. She shares my obsession with space, so she sided with me. (Don't criticize my family. Just because my dad likes fashion and my mom is interested in a things like space travel and being a doctor, doesn't mean we're weird.)

My sister and my dad finally moved, and I watched the greatest moment in history. Neil Armstrong walked on the moon! My mind was full of amazement, even though I had seen it before.

The next day, I went to school. I am 12 years old and in seventh grade. All of the kids (besides my best friend, Anthony) think I'm a nerd. They can think whatever they want; I don't really give a rap about it.

I spent my recess in the bathroom with the school bully, Derik Tinker. He gave me my weekly swirly down the toilet. I've told my teachers about him, but they never believe me. They think that he's a perfect little princess who earns straight A's.

(He only makes such good grades because the real class nerd, Jeff Hagworth, made a deal with Derik. The deal is that Jeff has to do Derik's homework and give him all the right answers on all of the tests. If he doesn't, Derik will pants Jeff in front of the whole school. Some deal.)

So there you go. That's one typical day of school.

As soon as school was finished, I invited my best friend, Anthony, to sleep over. Both of our moms were fine with it. Anthony knew how I really wanted to go to the moon, and he thought it was a pretty cool goal. He vowed he would work his butt off trying to help me achieve my potential.

When we got home from school, we were bored, and we wanted something to do.

"I have an ingenious idea," I said. "Let's make a YouTube video!"

"That's great!" said Anthony. "Let's make a video about you going to the moon, in honor of the broadcast yesterday!"

I have to give Anthony credit for his idea, because it was defiantly a good one. We found some cardboard in my garage and cut it into a 2-D rocket ship. Then we measured my head so we could build a 3-D space helmet for me. When we finished making our props, we borrowed my dad's camera and started recording.

Anthony introduced me to YouTube while I tried to look cool with that goofy piece of cardboard on my head. I went on the "stage" where our rocket ship was, which was actually a blank wall in my kitchen. I said a bunch of lame nonsense, and then at the last minute of the five-minute video, I jumped onto the cardboard cutout of the moon.

When we finished recording, Max edited the video while I watched. He's sort of a computer freak, and I have to admit, the final video was pretty awesome. Anthony somehow made my voice sound cooler, and when I jumped off the stage onto the fake moon, he put me into slow motion. When I hit the floor, a circle of smoke rose around me and dramatic music started to play. It was pretty intense for a home movie.

The minute after we published the video, it had fifty views. We weren't sure how that happened, but we thought it was a good start. We went off and did other things for the rest of the afternoon, but we decided to check our view count before going to bed. At 9:00 PM we pulled up our video again, and you will never in a million years believe what happened.

We had seven million views.

We both nearly fainted. We didn't know if this was a prank or a joke, but we were in total shock.

"Look at the comments," whispered Anthony.

I scrolled down to the comment section, and my heart sank. The first one said, "Get off YouTube!" Another one said, "You stink!" As we browsed through the rest of the comments, though, we saw that overall they were positive. "You should do this for real!" came up a lot. Someone else said, "There's no rule that says a child can't go to space." That was encouraging. After we finished reading the comments (there were like a thousand of them), Anthony put some advertisements on our video so that we could earn money from the views.

Weeks and months went by, and people kept watching our video. More and more support for our idea poured in. I had a fan base, and I knew what I had to do. I had to become the first kid to ever step on the moon. All I needed was a rocket ship and a ton of money.

And I knew where to get it.

I invited Anthony over and told him my plan. "I'm going to go to the moon, Anthony!"

"I think you really have gone crazy over this," he said. "It doesn't seem practical for a 12-year-old kid to go to the moon."

"I'll give you half the money we raise."

"Never mind. Let's do it!"

We started making and uploading more videos and running advertisements next to them to help us earn the money for our project. After a few weeks and a lot of effort, we had made and edited 96 videos. Over the next month, we reached a total of two billion views. More and more people were hearing about my dream and encouraging me to make it come true.

The videos made us $6,000. Pretty decent, but definitely not enough to buy a rocket ship.

We made a few more videos, but we were running out of ideas. I was worried my goal of going to the moon was going to fizzle out and die.

"We'll never make enough money this way," Anthony said one day. "You know what we need to do?"

"What?" I asked.

"We need to get on the news. Then everybody will know about what we're doing."

I thought he was crazy, but Anthony spent three straight hours on the phone. I just watched from my beanbag chair. He made countless phone calls and talked to who knows how many people.

He kept referring to me as "the kid with the moon videos on YouTube. Yes, the ones with two billion views." It sounded like the people on the other end were taking him seriously. I started to believe he might actually get us on TV.

When he was done, he told me that he booked me on *Good Morning America* and *The Tonight Show*. I couldn't believe it! This was my chance to tell the whole world about my dream!

First I went on *Good Morning America.* It was really cool to have millions of people looking at me. I also got really nervous, especially when I started to talk to the host. I explained my project and asked for donations to support my mission. Checks started flooding in. Anthony and I made about $30,000. After *The Tonight Show* we made another $20,000. It was insane. I thought I had gone to heaven or was having a dream where nothing bad could happen. I pinched myself regularly just to make sure I was alive and on planet Earth. Those pinches felt almost too real. This was really happening.

Now we were at $50,000, which had to be enough money, right? I realized I needed to start hiring workers and buying materials to build my rocket. I called Anthony to see if he wanted to come over and start planning the next phase of our project, but he didn't pick up. It was just as well. I needed to take some time off and process everything that had happened.

I don't know if I told you this, but after dreaming about space, my second favorite thing to do is fish. Anthony doesn't really like it, but I love it. So when he didn't pick up the phone, I grabbed my fishing rod and my bait and went out to the river.

As soon as I reached my normal fishing spot, I saw another kid already there. He looked familiar, and I realized too late that it was Derik, the school bully!

He turned around and saw me. "Well, if it isn't the moon boy. You lose your rocket ship around here?"

"Go away," I said. "This is my fishing spot."

"Not anymore," he said. He grabbed my fishing rod and threw it into the river. "Now you can't fish, just like you can't go to the moon."

I wanted to kill him. That fishing rod had cost about $200. My parents would be sooooo mad if I lost it. I waded into the river to find it, and after ten minutes of swimming in freezing cold water, I finally located it on the muddy bottom.

As I dragged it back out of the river, making a point of coming ashore far away from Derik, the line suddenly went taught. I had caught a fish! I quickly started to reel the fish in.

"Ha!" I said out loud. "I *can* go fishing, and I *can* go to the moon!"

Maybe I was too happy, because at that moment Derik jumped out from behind a nearby tree. He must have followed me down the river. "I said get lost, nerd!" he said. He stole my fishing rod again and snapped it in half. "Let that teach you a lesson! No fishing, no moon. You'll always be a nerd!"

I wanted to fight him, but if I tried he would snap *me* in half. So I picked up the broken pieces of my fishing rod and ran home, hearing Derik laughing at me all the way.

As I approached my house, I saw Anthony knocking at the front door. I ran up to him and told him what happened.

"Sorry to hear that," he said. He looked a little too sad for what I'd told him, though.

"What happened?" I asked. "Is something wrong?"

"I read about how much money it actually costs to build a rocket."

My heart sank. "Are we at least close to having enough?"

He silently shook his head.

It does not cost $50,000 to build a rocket. I'm not going to tell you the actual amount, because you might faint.

Okay, okay, I'll tell you. It costs about $4 million. We were doomed.

Anthony tried to cheer me up by telling me that he would call NASA and talk to them. I said okay, but I didn't feel like hanging out anymore, so he went home.

The next day of school was terrible! Derik told everyone about how he broke my fishing rod, and word had gotten around about my fundraiser to go to the moon. Derik and a bunch of his friends came up to me, and he said, "Hey, astronaut, visit the moon lately?" They laughed at me for a whole minute. I felt so embarrassed. I hoped Anthony was able to get through to

NASA, or I would be the laughingstock of the whole school forever!

Anthony came to my house at around 5:30 that evening. He told me that he had called NASA, and they'd said that if we could come up with half the money, then they would pay the other half. I was so happy! At least this made our goal more reasonable. It was still a lot of money to raise, but we were probably the richest kids at school. There had to be a way for us to do it.

After school the next day, I was sitting at home watching TV, and the weirdest thing happened. An ad came on that said a contest was being held with a prize of two million dollars. The man behind the contest was named Dr. Arthur Katz, and he was famous for inventing the flu shot. I never got a flu shot, but I wasn't going to tell that to Dr. Katz.

The contest was that someone would be thrown one hundred soft pitches, and if they hit one out of the park, they would win the money. Two million dollars?! That would be a big step toward going to the moon! I started to think that this could really happen!

Then they said that the person who would hit the pitches would be the person who wrote the best poem about how much they liked school.

I was about to quit, because there is absolutely nothing good about school. But I couldn't just give up. I had to at least try.

I called Anthony over, and we spent the rest of the afternoon writing a poem to submit to the contest.

This is it:

The teacher passed out and fell right off her chair.

My classmates are crying and gasping for air.

The hamster is howling and hiding his head.

The plants by the window are practically dead.

There's gas in the class; it's completely my fault,

And it smells like a chemical weapons assault.

So try to remember this lesson from she[1]

Don't take a dump in the class, or you'll end up like me.

I'm just kidding. That wasn't really our poem. I'm not going to show you our poem because it is way too embarrassing. Trust me when I say that. I'll just say that we did not mean a single word in it, and leave it at that.

Weeks passed, and people donated more money

---

[1]the teacher

to our project, but it wasn't anywhere near enough to buy the rocket. We really, really needed to win that contest if we had a chance of fulfilling my dream. The time for submissions to the contest ended, but when I didn't hear anything, I started to lose hope.

It was an ordinary, bad, boring, miserable day of school, though I did well on my history test, when something amazing happened. I opened the mailbox when I came home, and there was a letter in there addressed to me.

It was from the contest. It said "Two Million Dollar Poetry and Baseball Contest" right there on the return address. I could barely breathe. I tore open the envelope and pulled out a piece of paper. It said that I had won the contest, and that I would be batting next week on Thursday at 4:00

PM. I screamed in excitement and ran inside to call Anthony.

When I finished yelling the good news to Anthony over the phone, he started to laugh like I'd said the funniest thing in the world.

"What the heck are you laughing about?" I asked.

After about two minutes of nonstop laughing, he finally said, "I put that letter in your mailbox! I didn't think you'd take it seriously."

"WHAT?!" I exclaimed. "Why would you do that?"

"You stole my chocolate pudding at lunch today. Now we're even." With that, he started laughing again.

I could have been mad at him, but he was right. I did steal his chocolate pudding. And I had to admit, it was a pretty good prank. "Okay," I finally said, "we're even."

We talked about the real contest and concluded that if we'd won, we would have heard something by now. "Oh well," Anthony said. "At least we tried."

"Yeah," I said. "That money would've been a big help, though."

The rest of the day was uneventful. Oh, except for this one thing.

At exactly 8:36 PM, someone else called. I ran downstairs and picked up the phone. "Hello?"

"Is this James Gibson?"

"Yes, who is this?"

"My name is Arthur Katz…"

I almost fainted. Arthur Katz was the guy hosting the big contest. Suspicious, I asked, "Is this a prank call, or is this really you?"

"It really is me, Mr. Gibson. I'm calling to tell you that you won the contest for the best poem. You'll be batting on Monday at 6:30 sharp at Jeff Trolling Field. Best of luck!"

I promised I would be there, and we hung up the phone. I knew that Jeff Trolling Field was in California, but fortunately I live in California. So I told my folks about the contest and they were very enthusiastic. They said that my Mom would drive Anthony and me to the field. Monday couldn't come fast enough.

I don't want to brag or anything, but I was the best player on my Little League team. I knew I had this contest in the bag.

After a dull and boring day of school, the time came. It was the day I would slam a homer and win two million bucks. Anthony came over at about 3:00. It was a long ride to the field, but it was definitely going to pay off big time. I could almost see myself walking on the moon.

When we arrived, there must have been a thousand people in the stands. I started to feel nervous. That was a LOT of people watching me. What if I didn't actually hit one of the pitches out of the park? That would be so embarrassing. Not to mention it would ruin my chances of buying a rocket ship. Thinking about how much was riding on this contest, I almost peed in my pants.

I'd brought my trusty Louisville Slugger with me, so I warmed up in the batter's box. I saw the pitcher warming up, too. He was a tall, thin man, and I didn't recognize him.

The starting time came, and my heart began pounding. The pitcher stood on the mound. I stood at home plate. There was a box of one hundred balls next to the pitcher. One hundred chances to make my dream come true. "Okay," I thought. "Let's do this." I took a deep breath and focused.

The first pitch looked good, so I took a nice rip at it. I made good contact, but the ball just bounced down the third base line. I started to get a sick feeling in my stomach. This might be harder than I thought.

On and on it went. I missed some pitches and hit some others, but none went anywhere near the edge of the field. I started to feel tired from swinging the bat so many times, but I kept going. I had to do this. I had to win this contest!

Finally we were down to the last ball. Number one hundred. The pitcher threw, and I saw the ball flying toward me as if in slow motion. This was it. My last chance.

I lifted my left leg, put it down, and took a wild rip at that ball. I heard a smashing sound and felt the bat connect to the pitch, but I didn't know how solid the hit was. All of the spectators went completely quiet. I could feel them watching the path of the ball with me.

It flew past the infield and soared over the out-field, heading for the back fence. I held my breath, watching it, trying to guess where it would land. Going…going…going…

Gone! It was out of there! Bam! I started jump-ing around like crazy, yelling my head off. I'd done it! I'd hit it out of the park!

My mom and Anthony came over and hugged me, and we were all screaming and pumping our fists in the air. I could hear the audience cheering in the background. Then out came Arthur Katz, carrying this enormous check for $2,000,000. He presented it to me, and I had Anthony help me hold it. After all, he'd helped me get this far.

"We did it!" Anthony exclaimed. "You're going to go to space!" I just couldn't believe it.

On the ride home I felt stunned about what I had just done. This was a huge accomplishment. Anthony was making plans for buying the rocket ship, but all I could do was sit there in shock. This was really happening.

When we got home, I ran upstairs and hid the check in my closet. Then I called NASA.

"Hi," I said when they answered, "this is James Gibson."

"We know who it is. You've been calling us for years."

"Oh. Well, I just wanted to tell you that..."

"It's okay. We heard about you on the news this morning and watched the contest on TV. Great hit, kid!"

I grinned. "Thanks!"

"So I guess this means you've got the $2 million. We're sending someone to your house immediately to collect the money so we can start work on your rocket. Congratulations, James! You're going to the moon!"

The next day at school, Anthony and I we were floating on air. We felt like celebrities. Everyone wanted to know the details of how we won the contest and how NASA was planning a moon launch for me. Our teacher, Mrs. Farrell, said that Anthony and I could tell the class all about it during sixth period. When the time rolled around, we went to the front of the classroom and began to speak. The other students were very excited that someone they knew was going to the moon.

It actually became kind of hard to live with all of the fame. Whenever I was just out walking or something, people would come up to me and ask for my autograph and want me to tell them the whole story. I couldn't even go to my fishing spot without being ambushed by people stalking me. I was getting sick of it. I guess it was pretty cool, but I started to wish the moon trip would hurry up and happen so that people would leave me alone.

My birthday came, and we had planned to go parachuting. Normally you have to be 18 to go skydiving, but since I was going into space, they made an exception for me. I only invited Anthony. On the car ride to the skydiving place, Anthony felt really nauseous and eventually threw up. It was disgusting, but he felt a little bit better, so we continued on our way.

When we arrived, there were three people in the air slowly drifting down. I was so excited. This would be my first taste of what it felt like to fly in space! We took the class for how to stand at the door of the plane and how to hold your arms and legs when you were falling. We were each jumping with a tandem skydiving instructor, so all we had to do was enjoy the ride. The instructors grabbed parachute backpacks, and we followed them to the plane. On the ride up, my instructor explained that he would open the door, and we would just jump out. After about thirty seconds, he would pull the cord, and the parachute would deploy. The instructors hooked us all up to the equipment, and we were ready to go. My instructor opened the door, and out we jumped, followed by Anthony and his instructor.

When we were falling, it was really cool to see the view from that height. Everything looked so small, and I knew it would look even smaller from space. The falling feeling scared me, so when the instructor pulled the ripcord, I was not really prepared for it. I got a little bit of whiplash, but it was worth it. I was nervous about how much scarier it would be to actually go up in a rocket, though.

We floated in mid-air for about five minutes until we hit the ground. My parents were waiting for me, and they asked how it was. I told them it was really fun, but a little bit boring during the part when I was just hanging there. I didn't tell them about how nervous I'd felt on the way down.

On our way home in the car, I fell asleep and had the weirdest dream. I was in the spaceship, about to go to the moon, when suddenly the ship exploded with me in it. I woke up shaking and terrified about going to the moon for real with NASA. What if something went wrong? What if I couldn't handle it? What if the fear I felt while parachuting was only the beginning? I didn't tell anyone about the dream. I didn't want NASA to change their minds about sending me to space.

I had the same exact dream again that night. In the morning, I was just as freaked out as I was the day before. I couldn't keep it to myself anymore. I told Anthony the dream, and he told me to just forget about it. I decided he was right and tried to put the fear out of my mind.

At school we had an assembly about how obesity can affect your life in bad ways. Afterwards, they gave out ice cream. So it was another ordinary day.

Anthony called and told me that NASA kept sending him updates on the progress of my rocket ship. The ship would be ready in about a month, so I needed to go to a NASA simulator in Houston, Texas to try the space simulator. They said that they would pay for my transportation, which was nice. After all, I'd paid $2 million for the rocket.

When we arrived at NASA, it was pretty hot out. They gave us a tour, and I got to see the people working on my spaceship. Sparks were flying as machines welded sheets of metal together, and all of these people were running around, working hard to make sure the ship was ready on time. It was amazing to watch.

A tall woman walked up to us and told us that she worked for NASA and was very excited to meet my family and me. We walked into the main building. It was really cold in there, but I didn't care. I was too excited (and nervous) to try out the simulator. I had to prove I could handle the launch and the feeling of floating around in space. I had to prove it to NASA and to myself.

The simulator looked like a big ball with a bunch of straps. On one side of it there was a control panel with something like a hundred buttons. I climbed in and they strapped me inside. The tall woman said the first test was to see if I could handle the rumbly vibrations and G forces when the ship took off. I took a deep breath and nodded. Time to get serious.

They pressed a button, and suddenly I started vibrating and feeling my stomach fly down into my toes. It was completely insane. It felt like a rollercoaster in that chair.

It was also awesome. I started to think that maybe this whole rocket launch wouldn't be so bad.

After about a minute, the vibrations stopped. They said that the next test was to see if I would get motion sickness while hanging upside down in the ship. After feeling the force of a rocket launch, I didn't think this part could be too bad.

The person pressed another button, and I saw how wrong I was. I started flipping around in every direction, over and over and over again. I thought I was going to puke, but I squeezed my eyes shut and forced myself to hold it in. I had to get through this, or I could say goodbye to my dream of going into space.

It felt like forever, but they finally let me off the chair so that I could go to the bathroom. I could barely walk, but I was proud of myself for not throwing up. "At least I never have to go near that crazy simulator ever again!" I thought.

When I came back out, the woman had a serious look on her face. "Well, that didn't do so well on the second test. I'm afraid you'll have to re-take it."

My jaw dropped. Did I just hear that? I had to do it AGAIN? "Uh, do I have to?"

"We have to make sure you'll be safe on the launch. If you don't do it again, there's no way we can send you into space."

I was scared, but I nodded. "Can I just lie down for twenty minutes? Then I'll do the test again."

She said that was okay, so I found a row of chairs and lay down. I didn't get much real rest, and my stomach didn't even settle down because I was so nervous. After twenty minutes, I was returning to living hell. I don't think anybody could relax with that knowledge.

When it was time, I walked back over to the simulator. I was sweating. They strapped me in, and I almost peed in my pants. I felt like I was going to die. I closed my eyes and said, "Let's get it over with."

The woman pushed the button to start the test, and I tried to imagine myself in space. I wasn't on this crazy death machine. I was floating through my rocket ship, looking out at the earth and the moon and the stars. I started to calm down, and I knew that I could get through this. This was my dream, and I was going to make it happen.

I'm not going to tell you what happened in the restroom after that was over, but it starts with throw and ends with up. I felt much better after all of that food came out. I did get that gross feeling after you throw up, but I was okay. I'd made it through.

The woman said that I'd passed the second test,

and that NASA would see me in three and a half weeks for the launch.

After I went home, it turned out I was now national news. The front page of our newspaper said, in bold letters: **Youngest Space Traveler, James Gibson, Takes on Moon**. And the *New York Times* said: **James Gibson, To Infinity And Beyond**.

It was cool to be famous. At school I was even more popular then before. Even the other kids wanted my autograph. They probably just wanted to sell it when I came back from the moon, but whatever. It was nice to know that everyone wanted to be me. Even that bully Derik was leaving me alone for once. Maybe he just didn't want to be in the news for beating up the world's youngest astronaut.

After three and a half weeks, it was the day before I was going to the moon. I was so excited that I had trouble falling asleep that night. Everything was coming together. My life was so perfect, I could hardly believe it!

Eventually I did fall asleep, and I had that same nightmare from the day I went parachuting—a nightmare of being trapped as my rocket ship exploded around me. I woke up screaming and scared. I was starting to believe it wasn't just a dream; I had never had three of the same dream before. What if it was a warning? What if this wasn't a good idea? What if I was getting everything I wanted in life, only to lose it all?

"Just forget about it," I said to myself. "It's just a dream."

Still, I couldn't go back to sleep.

The launch was happening in Florida. The

plane ride over there was really cool for about thirty seconds, and then it got really boring. I was on a private plane because if I'd gone on an ordinary plane, I would have been crowded by people asking me for autographs, and it would have been crazy.

We arrived at the launch pad, and I tried to forget all about my fame, my fears, and my nightmares. I was about to go into space. I couldn't afford to think about anything else. There were three people going with me—the pilot, the captain, and one other person who was going to watch me and make sure I brushed my teeth and ate healthy food and all of that garbage. I was kind of mad, because I'd thought I would get the chance NOT to do all of that, but at the moment I was too excited about the launch to worry about it.

We climbed into the rocket, and I turned to say

goodbye to my family. My parents were hugging me and kissing me and checking to make sure I'd packed everything I needed. Mission Control said, "James Gibson's shuttle, we are going to launch in about five minutes." The pilot said my parents had to leave right away. As the door to the ship closed, my mom and dad told me to be safe and waved and cried and blew kisses through the window.

What else can you expect from your parents when you're about to go to the moon?

They cleared the launch area, we strapped into our chairs, and the countdown started.

Ten…

I felt my heart starting to race.

Nine…

Images from my nightmare flashed through my mind.

Eight…

What if something went wrong?

Seven…

What if I got sick, and they decided we shouldn't go to the moon after all?

Six…

What if the rocket DID explode?

Five…

I closed my eyes and focused on my imagination. I thought about how amazing it would be to see space with my own eyes.

Four…

This was my dream. I couldn't back out now.

Three…

Even if it scared me, I was going through with it.

Two…

I opened my eyes.

One.

"Here we go," I whispered.

The next few seconds were crazy! We shot up into the air faster than the fastest rollercoaster in the world. It was like the simulator, times one thousand. A bunch of smoke and fire went everywhere below the rocket. I could see some of it out the window. I didn't have time to be scared, because the next thing I knew, I was in the air. The rest of the crew was cheering and clapping for me, and I guess one of them had unstrapped me from my chair so I could float around. I looked out the window again, and there was no more fire or smoke.

Instead, there were only stars.

All of my fear disappeared. I was the happiest person alive. Here I was, in a real space ship, going to the moon. No other kid in the world had gotten to do what I was doing right now.

After a while my body adjusted to the space ship, and I started learning what it was like to live in space. Once we were out of the atmosphere, we didn't have to wear our spacesuits anymore, so it was a lot easier to float through the ship. Dinner was freeze-dried chicken and orange juice, which tasted exactly the way it sounds. I also accidentally spilled the orange juice.

Normally when you spill orange juice, or any other liquid, it falls to the ground because of gravity. When I spilled the juice in space, it just floated in midair in little spheres. So I drank it from the air. It was so cool. I spilled the rest of it on purpose so I could drink it the same way.

I missed my parents and Anthony, and even my sister, but I had bigger things to worry about. I was about to become the first kid ever to walk on the moon.

The night after we launched, I had another dream. Instead of landing on the moon, my ship crashed on another planet—one that scientists had never discovered. I went out to see where we were, and one of the local aliens asked me for a dollar. When I gave it to him, he gave me ten billion dollars. I woke up confused, but I was glad that I didn't have that same scary dream again.

In the morning the pilot told me that we would arrive on the moon in about forty-six more hours. I was really excited about that. I couldn't wait to get there!

The next two days were surprisingly boring. The spaceship was kind of cramped, and there wasn't a lot to do except wait to arrive on the moon.

One unexpected thing did happen. There was a huge—and I mean HUGE—meteoroid storm.

We were all worried that one would go right through the window and we would all be crushed. Luckily, we survived without too much damage. The ship was hit a few times, but the damage was small enough that we could fix it on the moon. We made it out alive, and the ship seemed fine, so we kept going.

A few hours after that excitement, I happened to look out the window and saw the moon in a way I had never imagined it.

It was…big. You don't realize how big things are in space until you get to see them up close. The moon was huge—nothing like the little circle I had seen at home when I looked up at the sky. It grew bigger and bigger as we approached its surface.

When you land on an airplane, you just get a

little bump. The spaceship landing was more of a crash. I thought we had wrecked the ship, but the pilot told me it was normal.

We suited up and got ready to go outside. We had to do a little jump from the ship's airlock to reach the moon's surface, so the captain counted down. One, two, three, and jump. When I jumped, I floated in the air for a few seconds longer than it would have taken on Earth. Also, when I hit the ground, a small cloud of dust rose around me. It looked like one of the videos that Anthony and I made to start this whole adventure. I reached down and touched the moon with my gloved hands, and it felt amazing. Then I looked straight up and saw Earth, hanging there in space. It looked like I could just pick it up.

We were doing a broadcast from the moon's surface, just like Neil Armstrong had done so

many years ago. The pilot started recording and let me talk for a while. I said that I was so happy, and that NASA was amazing for putting this together. I thanked everybody who had contributed money to the rocket, especially Arthur Katz for sponsoring the baseball and poetry contest. I also said how nice and supportive my parents were during this whole experience. Last, but definitely not least, I thanked Anthony for all of his hard work. This was our project, and we had made it happen.

After I said all of that, the pilot moved the camera towards the view of the Earth. I couldn't believe how many people were watching me— probably millions. After the broadcast was over, I picked up a moon rock to bring back with me. I knew that the moon rock would be very valuable back on Earth, and now that I'd put all of my money into buying the spaceship, it would be good to have something to sell when I got home. W e climbed back into the ship and took off from the moon to return to Earth. I was incredibly happy to be me right then. I was definitely the luckiest kid alive.

After only about five minutes, we crashed into something. It felt like we'd landed back on the moon. None of the other people on the ship knew what had happened.

We tried to open the door, but it was stuck. We really needed to get outside to figure out what was going on, so we all put on our spacesuits, the pilot grabbed a hammer, and he broke the door down.

We walked outside into an amazing place. Everything burst with color. It almost looked like a cartoon, but the people we saw walking around were real. They were also breathing, so we took off our spacesuits and walked around in our normal clothes. A short while after we got out of the ship, these two people walked up to the pilot and me and told us to come with them. We didn't know what else to do, so we obeyed.

We were eventually led to their king, who wanted to know who we were and how we had come to his planet. We started talking about

Earth, and eventually the king saw a dollar bill in my pocket. He looked like he was about to pass out with wonder. He told me to take the money out of my pocket, so I did.

The next thing I knew, he was bowing to me. I was really confused. Wasn't he the king? Shouldn't we be bowing to him?

He said that he would trade me ten pounds of gold for the dollar. Now I felt like I was the one

who would pass out. This was straight out of the dream I'd had before the moon landing! I didn't know why he wanted the dollar so much, but I had no problem with the trade. Without hesitating, I gave him the dollar, and he gave me the gold. The pilot helped me carry it back to the ship.

When we returned, the ship was fixed! I have no idea how, but there it was. We climbed in, took off from the strange planet, and headed back to Earth.

When we landed, it was with a more pleasant bump than the one that had brought us down to the moon. I could hear a crowd of people cheering from a mile away. After I went through all of the procedures and tests and things you have to do when you come back from space, I was allowed to go outside.

Hundreds of people wanted to meet me and get my autograph. My parents were there, and they started hugging me and asking me questions and saying how much they missed me. Anthony gave me a high five and told me that I looked great up there on TV.

It took a few hours to talk to all of the reporters and sign all of the autographs, but we finally went back home, again on the private plane. I showed my parents the ten pounds of gold, and they almost fainted. They asked me, "Is that real?"

I said, "I really don't know."

When we got home, my parents found a gold appraiser, and we brought my gold to him. He inspected it and said that it was fake, which made it basically worthless. He said that he would give me a dollar for it anyway.

I took the dollar. I was a bit disappointed, but at least I wouldn't have to come home looking for thieves in my closet every night.

Later that night I was watching the news on the TV, and it showed the gold appraiser. The mayor was our town was standing next to him, congratulating him on finding the gold on a treasure hunt. He said that the gold was worth hundreds of thousands of dollars.

I was so mad! That guy had ripped me off!

The next day, the whole town knew about this guy. My parents and I went back to his shop to confront him. He was talking to the mayor on the phone, but when we walked in, he hung up immediately. My parents started to yell at him because of what he had done. He said that he didn't know that it was actually real until he checked it at his lab. I knew that he was lying; he had just wanted my money.

We called the police, and when they came in, the guy started to sweat and look tense. The police said that we would have to discuss this in court, so I had to wait to get my gold back.

The next day of school was fun. Normally I would never, ever say that school was fun, but that day was fun. In fact, if I had to write another poem about the best thing about school, I'd write about that day. As soon as I arrived, everyone crowded around me to get my autograph and to ask me about my trip. We actually skipped all of the learning that day, and instead we had three hours of recess and watched videos about the moon, including the broadcast I did while I was there. Everyone thought it was really cool to have someone in class who had been to space.

The day finally came when we were going to court with that loser who tricked my family and me into giving him the gold. It was kind of fun. We had a lawyer and everything. I got to speak, and my lawyer got to speak, and then the other guy and his lawyer got to speak.

I'm not going to tell you who won the case.

Okay, I'll tell you.

I did. The guy had to give me back the gold! I was the richest kid in school, and thanks to my moon trip, I was also the most popular.

When I was on the moon, I imagined it to be much more boring because the only time I'd seen it was on the Neil Armstrong video. But when I was on the moon, it was insane to be there. Earth looked like a peaceful environment with no war or anything bad happening. Just a moving ball of different colors.

Now that I had been to the moon, I didn't know how life could get any better. Unless, of course, I went to Mars.

But that's a different story, so you have to pay for that one separately.

CPSIA information can be obtained at www.ICGtesting.com
Printed in the USA
BVOW03s0154210414

351145BV00002BA/51/P